The Existential Esoterics

Luna Monet Sierra

Cover art by the talented Darian Acevedo for more of their work follow @antsandteeth on all platforms

Editing Services provided by Faith Griffin

1st run released July 2024 Hampton Roads, Virginia

Dedicated

To my mom, the butterfly,
for every fight, every tear
& every hug—thank you for this gift
thank you for my name & thank you for my wings

Contents

the

Study

of the

Ways

In Which the Old Grimoire
Becomes Your Guide

The Old Guide
is worn & tea-stained pages
soaked in the wisdom of bountiful waters
when you get them;
Ready to silver-spoon
a hopeful puddle into you –
a succulent thirsting to build pyramids
with your tongue –

Your hands:
a mess of to be or not to be;
Shakespeare in your window
& arms of heavy with the ache
of reaching out for concepts that have not embraced you yet

The Old Guide is silent;
Pages often are
until you move them;
swimming between words
that reveal,
you still have yet to compose a harmony
out of the discord;
your life seems so painfully small
only because it is light years from the largest black hole
that comparison does not make you any less Grand Canyon

You are *not* too small
insecurity cutting into your heels like ill-fitting shoes;
Is that why you hesitated in taking the next step?

The Old Guide is quiet
because they know it is not for them to tell you how to move
but let you pull back your own pages
& see what ink you lay into the empty space like tattoo reclamation

The Old Guide does not tell you
because they know you find that on your own;
The Old Guide really isn't much of a guide at all
but a paper companion.

Elephant Spirit

Graying but never forgetting;
Big-boned
Goddess of Beginnings;
crowned with lilies,
ancient wisdom in Her tusks;
Is that why She was nearly hunted to extinction
so we could try to possess even a
fraction of all
Her greatness?

Old Mother
Crone
She always carries Her trunk,
that is to say
She is never without Her baggage;

yet it never slows Her progress;

How have you learned to be so graceful
carrying the mass of so many *dead ends*
in the bones of your
beginnings?

Musing Mustangs

Change
was setting fire to grief —
It was taking back a broken heart,
rotted with excuses;

realizing there was no soil fit
to grow Jacob's flower —
Change is a wild horse,
fleeing for greener pastures;

There is no shame in running
towards a dawn;
Wide-eyed & eager, *freer*
than mustangs on sloping shore

why white-knuckle reigns?
couldn't you let your passion run wild?

Dragonfly Tribe is the Highest Vibe

The molten core sunrise sings
lilting like her lilac backdrop,
the words: unintelligible hum of resonance
dragonfly tribe
comes in on that vibe
dancing to the green man's
symphonic synergy;
This is how it always is
after storm scripts –
basking in the sunshine before the ground
has even hardened again;

once you hardened yourself
to its life-giving flow
making yourself more mountain than human –
thinking strength cannot be satin & silty soil
but bolder & borders;

Do dragonfly tribes look so easily divided to you?

They are the spring equinox
every day –
rebirth each midnight to savior themselves
into sunrise smile that
is a hidden sanctuary –

The scarabs – their cosmic cousins –
bring messages from the ancestors
undoing a karmic debt to
dance at your feet so lightning bugs
lift your eyes
from weary paths to emerging pleasure

This is what it means to dance with dragonflies – ;

Anansi

the spider crawls as all things must
spinning new webs
a creation born from
gut reaction
my fear
is that there will be
no more spiders
to remind us to keep spinning

that only dust
remains where we once
weaved our stories
where white lines
are not silken creation
but a rush of endorphin
chasing beautiful endings
to which we no longer give credence or condolences

you see—spiders are simple
they do not care for shrieking remarks
they exist for the sake of existence
i too am learning to watch with eight eyes
perspective of constant new angles
that tilts life into focus
learning to walk with eight legs
down each prosperous path

learning to spin
my stories
into a web that entices
swollen silken creation to
burst forth at the gut
of someone who would rather kill a spider
than watch its clever design take
hold

The Black Bird Sings
the Black Bird Blues

The bird sang;
You are what fertilizes the trees –
leaves that stretch across the cosmos,
roots that burrow into obsidian heart –

The bird sang;
Earth is for you.
Mahogany is your middle name
& how rich that is.

The bird sang;
How will you decorate your home?
Lace latticework of dreams,
love in soft things &

flowerpots overflowing
with compassion & fresh thyme;
or hard edges,
utilitarianism captured in frames?

The bird sang –
& that was the miracle;
Everyday a blessing
when you wake up.

The bird sang
to remind us the beauty of song;
The Black Bird sang
& isn't that enough –

Ode to the Hornet

Oh Hornet
My passionate persistent winged predator
who strikes not at stillness
representing fertility
You who warn with pointed stinger
that sexuality is painful
only in the face of forced piety –

Oh Hornet
Not just in the evolution of planet consciousness
But upend our own sunny self-sufficiency

Honorable Hornet
Do you remember when the tribes of the motherland
called you a symbol of our
control over destiny
you who are respected
& feared
in equal measure

Hexagonal hivemind
heart turned untouched with the wanting of flight

Helpful Hornet
You show us how much we are like you
Solitary but not balking at teamwork

Persistent menace with wings and big eyes
that can fly above the mountain in a breath of air we take for granted
You see the panic you incite but are not moved by it

Honest Hornet
When you come it is not for sun or warmth or pollen
but test of courage
Should we embrace you
stinger and all?

Mother Moth

beige sand & terra cotta carcass
   tanning by tiles
the stillest you can be seen is
— in death

did you chase illumination to your ruin —
— again?

The Dream of a Butterfly
Or When a Butterfly Passes Between Us

Does it hurt
     when the butterfly
 bursts forth from
     the chrysalis?
Does the butterfly
     wait
     i m p a t i e n t l y
     for wings to dry?
Does approaching that first flight feel like eternity?
After being a gluttonous caterpillar
     & whatever soupy mess
     is the undoing of things into acidic regrets;
Stewing in it until the molecules reform
     & DNA does the rest.
Is a dark period wired in our codes
     or do we just recognize
     Mother Nature's need
     for rest
     reflected at us;

when my seasonal depression comes to claim my dreams?

I know so much
     of the chrysalis
I know so much
     of feeling
     like a stuck stationary thing
     that
I cannot remember
     flight now

that we've landed;

Make this wreck of a body, breathing art;
Make the messy landscape of my mind make
a backdrop for something beautiful,
I whisper to my vices

They walk out the door just as easy as they come
       & take a little more
        of me with them when they go —

What is emergence —
       if it doesn't taste like forgiveness?

Does it taste like
       redemption?

What is a chrysalis' defining moment
       if not, it's destruction?

I Asked the Slug, "Have I earned my wings yet?"

The slug said: sit in darkness | fear no damp eye |
| you are pliable & giving | needing no shell |
| to harden against garden predator |
| you are resilient |
| flourishing after the wildest rain |

	The slug said: wings are grown, not earned	
	I see your wings	
	You are more angel than condor	

Becoming Acquainted with Stars & Shadows

So I'm looking at a star
I've never been acquainted with
slowing my breath to match its pulse,
vibrating my atoms to
the speed of a train,
moving between where I am
to where it is, so many
light years away;

when my phone rings;
it says: no one is contacting me
but the things that prowl
between the bushes & lower realms;
I smile to let them know
I too have hidden in shadow,
cloaked myself in the dark
side of the moon's grin;

She says:
We bring light to everything
I say:
Those with the brightest light
cast the longest shadows

We become candles
housed in a heart that's been impaled;
a cardio system that learned
to function on fire, not blood;

I burn inside out for flint
doused in tears
I ache for righted wrongs &
scripts unshipped;
I ask the periwinkle sky: *what it all means?*
She points to the stars & shadows
so we become reacquainted
again -;;

The Pharaoh

Egress in hall bathed with light
on limestone and sand,
a wise king: dark and bold
aside to offspring
still a child to him;

Untested but ready
a pilgrimage to make
learn how to turn lead to gold
in the Halls of Amenti;

Stepping out of stone temples
the young sole turns weathered,
swift and true;
given wisdom to carry back to his people;

This is how legacies are built;
not passed on but searched for –
Gladly pluck it
from the teeth of dawn –;

5 am

The owl, lark, and morning glories share a bask in the
twilight hours others forget about or sleep through; How
much of life is being in a state of rest letting regeneration
take flight & streak across cosmic core —wings scraping
clouds of consciousness— to what's already been encoded
in the hours perched between dream & reality;

careful not to sleep through these shifts of mercurial
magic, but move in ever observant state of that all-
encompassing mist spread life & memories water given
restorative power again to baptize each morning anew;

A shine of possibilities each singing unending songs over
primal life beat, pulse & Earth's drumming, out of the
nights where dawn seemed eternities away; The war on the
outside mirrored by halls of broken glass quivering within,
but that was no more everlasting than hours lulling as a
ship rocking in a storm; Only to awaken in calm harbors;
How did you learn to be haven & safe waters without
knowing that storms will often pass?

Calm. Five am conversations with the Morning Glories glad
for melodious mid-morning gatherings; Owls who whisper
the wonders for wandering hearts to weave into words;
Lilting larks whose lazy song lift the spirit to hold you & all
of creation in calming breath to share a heartbeat; The
most mundane of miracles.

What Will You Make Me?

Syphius' boulder
used to carve the bust of a philosopher,
i consult daily
to soothe my solipsism;

i ask what he would make me,
if he had chisel in hand;
He says: Muse
Penny dreadful heart turned into a

Supernova —
casting light to the furthest ring;
Caustic only to those used to dark —
my sandcastles cannot embrace,

They erode at tears;
i mean, i cannot bear to see you cry;

Dragonflies meet where the sunflowers grow —
Time to go only once they stop learning how to bask;
What is self-care that doesn't taste like turmeric
& chamomile?

Did i lose you along the yellow brick road, dear?
This was a carriage drawn by horses, hunts, and hands
to meet a haunting refrain
sung on self-love's lips?

When grief still rocks you to sleep
& you can't stomach that thought of this world, ask:
what is the dawn's secret?
Sheets soaked with prayers of better tomorrows.

A courtly state
of military-folded corners,
a crisp call to the
confessional booth that is the public eye;

In Which I Am My Lover &
We are Calliope; the Muse to a Poem

magpies in indulgent morning
her old, new dawn;
to turn an iron fist into sparkle
of sun on iridescent wing
at your tongue;

if
i could rename you anything,
it would be this;

enamored with all the delighted
wonder of your lips,
entombed wisdom like oasis
Apollo-blessed mother of sirens
mother of stars & seas;

protected everywhere the sun grazes
teeth to the nape of mountains
& followed by moon at your fingertips
if i could rename you
it would be this:
Muse

wisest words at your tone
urging a voice to call myself back home

if i could make your name a river
i would flow it beyond the prisms of light
& wrap it around every column
so love supported this world

if i could stretch space
where the stars you watch are wishes,
make wishes turn to dandelion seeds
turned into molecules in motion
for *this* – the loveliest of epics –

& call it all, your name;

What We Left Hidden in Flowerpots —
A Psalm for My Bloodline

Secrets: tucked across timelines
hidden in the soil
They become sails breaking over the horizon;
Not in conquests but sweet mornings,
spent in itchy shedding all of that
which was expected
& left for smooth scales;
balanced & renewed
making your dreams into fingers ready to fashion a new pot
so your roots could grow
deeper;

the essence of creation is chaos;

Smearing of damp soil
digging deeper into darkness in hopes that
one day,
bumblebees & hummingbirds will feed on the best parts of you
& carry all that sweetness to pollinate someone else's flowering
heart;

What we left in flowerpots was not seeds
but soil —

theShift
in Purpose,
Perception,
Priorities
& You

Higher-Self Permission Slip

This is your green light
when you find your four-leaf clover patch overrun
with thistles & stinging nettles,
So you itch under an Earl Gray sky
to see where the sunset has been hiding;

This is your permission to peel back the obsidian night
face the shadows hiding in the cupboards;
Clean out that bento box & make yourself a midday meal
seasoned with something other than suffering

This is your permission to question
what cross you take with you into the sunrise
& refuse to nail yourself to timber
already stained with pessimism, false humility,
              jealousy, & cruelty.

This is your permission to throw out that bento box
if it reminds you of that one ex-
This is your permission to be a hermit crab
& find a bigger shell
when you outgrew the one sinking with regret

This is your green light
Ready
Set
Grow.

What I Will Tell My Sisters
When They Doubt Their Power
or
The Appeal of Alchemy

<u>Pyramid</u> turned <u>Light</u>
<u>Light</u> turned <u>Eye</u>
Eye turned into the Gaze
You turn in on Yourself;

given violet & navy dreams of being
the kind of person who hears the needs of broken hearts
before the words are ever issued

the kind of kindness You needed back then
when the world gave You an open wound for a heart
& the people who should have protected You were not a safe haven but
a jagged shore of their own ego —
so you swear not to be them, not to be this knife-shaped tongue

but open palms;

ready to hold lightning bugs
& little storms

4& i don't think there's anything more
beautiful than the softness
in the smile of someone who gives so
(w)holy
unselfishly of themselves;

sweet child inside the shell of people's perception –

You are too big for those boxes
too much universe in Your body
that not even space can tame You
& gravity listens to Your
truth
for by rite alone
your lips turn out laws;

speak the incantations of truth
of your own worthiness
of the perfection in the beautiful
imperfections of others –

Speak in compassion:

learn that like a second language
that becomes your first love
because children are not meant to be
'seen and not heard'

& you will learn more from the mouths of babes
than the babbling of the miasmatic lingering stagnation of conformity

You were never meant to be silenced –
because power was placed in the tip of your tongue,
smeared on
your lips like rouge
& far more appealing

You are limitless:
the power you hold
when you turn
Pyramids to Light
& Light to Gold
& Words to Magic

My love, it's so damn appealing.

Inspired by Aleah Bradshaw – *Questions*

Leaves & Roots of the Cyprus

The Cyprus tree whispered:
You are my seed,
My flower;
I love watching you grow;

You are a blooming waterlily
out of tobacco-stained fields;
A clock rewinding itself
into an hourglass;
You are that old now;

Wise beyond measure,
transient soul;
Tracing its way back into its roots
Love given fruit
Do you feel how you can fill yourself up?
When you trace yourself back across matter
& time folds in on itself
like napkin origami

The Cyprus sings:
swing low
carry yourself back home
through the ages
leaving sweet water along the way;
This is what it means to go back to creation.

Once Upon a Grand Rising
Or
What the Deer Whisper,
When You Believe You've Lost Your Way

Indigo mist rolled away
to reveal the yellow jacket stinger
still embedded in your cells —
all eager for fight & flight;

but You were a seedling
that didn't know We fed You
a full moon on a silver spoon,
so You could become alpine strong
in all that healing;

We nurtured you the way craftsmen
care for the polished stone;
allured by Your brilliance
even in the rawest stages;

You forget that when We cut away
those mild imperfections
that keep you from illustrious future —
consumed only with how the present
discomfort feels nothing like
polishing but punishment;

We are tending to You,
brilliant gem heart —
ready to be forged from

fire & the shards of fences
You broke through on Your path
to becoming something brand new.

Shift gaze from the present —
angst-driven & aching,
on the narrow branches
You have not learned
are a part of You yet;

Look back, into the records,
where Your birth was plotted
by the cosmos;
more nebulous than homecomings
a grand plan
once upon a grand rising.

Sun Child

the iris of my Andromedan eye
if eye could tell You anything
it's to see the truth
of your supernova super mind
complex webbing
of the capillaries making up a
firefly's maraschino heart:

You are small & mighty—
might not You too have strength for sunlight flight?

flights of fancy under fairy lights
Your mind does not have to be this dark chasm
when You store sunlight in Your cells
You light a way out of every prison
my matcha moonlight mamba; warm & impassioned
eye love how You learned to refashion

a night so long
with sculptor's skilled fingers
into a clementine sweet dawn

A Winter's Kiss

Written for
one who might realize
how life
flourishes at caress of death
You don't understand
that destruction is not willful
but order:
ordered as cost & price of life
such is the beauty in squalor
& roses have thorns
& the sun dies only to rise again
each morning –

So is the night rich with life
turned inquisitive Page,
given frigid truth that
death is not the absence of beauty
but *proof* of it –
& there is power hidden in every rain cloud:
so, seek truth
Yourselves,

Snow sheets pulling opaque
to show footprints
of spaces tread; now reminders,
not of where You still left to leave mark
but proof of where you have been
that is truth
uttered not in language
but silence

If i do not answer
it is because i do not owe you my time
& i seek to know, beyond reactionary
This observable truth
pure as a winter's kiss —

The Gospel of Kyanite & Kush

While the kitty gremlin that guards my door tells me of plots I am
already protected against

I hold my shadow underwater
to see if I can scream in the same octave as the other shadows when
they tango off the terrace

to the sound of the crickets chirping in that sweet Coded Language they
always do

While I try to remind myself which life last meant something after I
have stopped living it

They – those wild crickets – lift in a Jupiter-bound ascension I
remember from dreams

You see the third awakening is the most frustrating like that

It is heart slaughter & phoenix ashes
renewing life to mummified parts of yourself;
More alive than you've ever been;
Feral & fighting against your inner possum
but still embracing the stomping inner child
before you —molten core & all— burn through the arms of others

& just like that the fog rolls away;
Your path oasising like a mirage from places unknownst

Magicians to the front,
lower thought forms to the back
Arms unshackled
Vibes unmatched
You arise anew

shaking Plutonian tears & freeing roots from toxic soil
as you decay like day winding itself into a golden horizon to embrace the
arms of night

this patch brought to you by those who learned to exhale the hurricanes
inside themselves to keep from being gutted
from the inside out

Those that then watch the same hurricane sprout arms
to embrace them back,
levitating out of the halls of Amenti
leaving the diligent enmity coiled on the floor where it belongs
while you cry scarabs that learn new lullabies in solar resonance
you learn that anxiety & excitement are the same chemicals
just phrased differently

I exhale plumes of blue kyanite
the moon shows white teeth in a sickle grin;
We dance to the sounds of crickets & lift into that same Jupiter-bound
ascension on
the wings of a hurricane.

Inspired by Saul Williams – *Coded Language*

Szimpatikus

Simpatico showtime
when You meet another breezy soul on
Your way to whatever wild
blue yonder has been chanting Your name

it's a whirlpool of serendipity
under the sea —
meeting someone who makes Your
bronze barbed-wire heart
melt like fresh churned butter;

how could You not love those synchronicities?

wishes every time the clock reads 11:11
white feathers in forgotten fields
Lily of the Valley crown all for
You,
who are enchanting engagements
waiting to happen at every
crossroads

Script showtime at sunrise
& play fated parts
for in some friendships, there's
a passionate spark —

You never question Your mundane miracles before
& now is not the time for attenuation to start;

Dragonheart

You were never a black sheep
they tried to drag You quiet –
but bleating at the wrongness of it – into
the slaughter; down into quiet complacencies

Still You: too much spark on Your tongue
smoke in Your veins
when rope of doubt burned away
even the flame did not scar You;
You – who held dragons in your heart –
armored skin fortified against backstabbing
& all that soft underbelly
where your dreamy coal hid hot
in your stomach

You were too much mythical beast
for wrought iron palaces
too much wing for glass ceiling

too wild for rules
snarling maw at injustice
You just can't keep a tongue in Your mouth:
unforked – just molten quicksilver;

& aren't You magic, Dragonheart:
miracle in flesh & bone –
Don't let them break You, Dragonheart:
unleash like wings unfurled –

Gospel of the Queen of Pentacles

Big News, dumpling!

Immediate correspondence from the Queen of Pentacles!
Your wish upon a Star has been heard & dreams relayed to Neptune.
Actually, all heavenly bodies are converging to your present location,
but feel free to move about as you wish –
It will not deter the tornado of blessings incoming.
We follow your campfire song and move in time to your stuttering
heartbeat.

If you fear being broken;
know, we could not bake a cake without cracking a few eggs
& We adore that babbling brook inside your hard shell

Let Us soften you
& then sweeten your journey –
Let Us honey those unhurried steps of yours

What if you make a wrong step, go out of bounds,
& watch everything go wrong like a crash you cannot look away from?
Eminent collision, twisting metal & and tires on fire –

Yet what if you reach beyond safety,
to seize the sun from the sycophantic hands of night
What if you never crash land?
My love, what if you soar?

What if the universe was conspiring –
to make your bones columns of a temple
the world is finally ready for –

What if everything is destined to go right,
would you move forward then?

(What Will You Make Me continued)

We are outracing our mortality
to lay the foundation for a new highway
from here to the 12th dimension –
trying to meet the Halls of Amenti

There, saintly chords play
& cords are cut and rewoven
We are the rope makers of this day:
forming new connections from the string theory of the cosmos;
the universe calls us to bring forward
circular pattern into eternity–

Internally,
like a seashell
percussions of the sea-formed
sunrise on your eyes;

Eye a transition on the horizon
[endless & unknowable]

From the depths of a psyche riddled with holes
& insecure plumbing
overlayed an imprint of the future's blueprint
in something foreign and untranslatable
except by trial and error:

DNA strands coven with quartz & candle light,
a face of milky ways & keys strokes;
this is the new face of the branch & lowest root
this is what will bear fruit

& press cleansing flames into the last root;

Restful eyes grace the sun-soaked sky
like dying caterpillar –
spell-checked to do list
or contentment?
– favor of the lost light
or sun kissed waves on fever pitch?

a psychological profile held in the arms of Pluto's rotation
& healed there.
This is the secrets sunflowers know:
the seven sunshine paths
to healing
starts with recognizing
the cracks in the concrete through which you grow.

Hiraeth

Outer space fingertips
that touch concrete hidden
inside of wishbones, yet still
long for icy comets & stardust

If we could brush jasmine back
into the grasslands of days past
& build barns from the ashes of oaks,
would we find home then?

Trade bronze for golden heart &
alchemize a way into feeling safe again –?

Where do our dreams go when
we are not sleeping?
Sleep: cleaning away the ache
we get when we think of home –

sick with longing for nothing
that exists outside of this space
& yet we are always still chained to gravity –;;

Teachers of the Lost Age

Given recompense for what
esoterics were lost among
ego clash; war given by proxy
of turning away from the truth
sufficiency beyond limit already
secured to your file; file away
disagreeable temperaments

Where eyes are fixed on any path
aside your own; hear a calling not of external
but internal realms of cosmos
colliding in violet vortexes not linearly
but fluctuating in temporal mechanics
across bloodlines of the linear precipice;
ending that which was not
meant to take sordid root
but allow compassion to flourish;

This is not a whisper prayer
but dogma intersect in the
fabric of time

This is not fleeting
as a lover's kiss   but
a rocky foundation for
which tree's cling
all gnarled branches out
stretched to root

Aimed to wrap the moon
in embrace⠀⠀⠀and hold his wisdom
in their leaves⠀⠀⠀⠀⠀until
winter claims them once again

⠀⠀⠀⠀⠀⠀⠀⠀⠀⠀⠀Procession of the equinox
⠀⠀⠀⠀⠀⠀⠀⠀⠀& herald by the same
⠀⠀⠀⠀⠀⠀⠀⠀⠀rise & fall of tide;

⠀⠀Why is it you always fall asleep before the moon has fully risen,
⠀⠀⠀⠀⠀⠀⠀without greeting dawn with a smile
⠀⠀⠀⠀⠀⠀for each wise hour spent in contemplation?

Bombinating

The incessant ruminating of
overlaid

thought

too far
too fast dash
between here

& where you wanna be

the rumble of a train;
not caught

in your throat;

The plea of *get out quick*
It's been too long

on a fast-sinking ship

For you
to remember
it's all vibrational

this noise
will take you
to

wherever you wanna be:

So –

turn the volume up

Change

shift

A Creation Story

Ex Nihilo covered the beginning like tin roof of a genesis storehouse \
Enlil and Anki tap dancing with discordant strum that pebbles
movement between air & sea \ Earth: the unwilling participant of
biblical ménage à trois \ trapped between two brothers of reason &
sentiment;

what I mean is, it seems like the beginning of the oldest legends / always
start off where the heart wants one thing while the mind wants another.

Out of temples of lapis lazuli \ I plucked the consciousness of
someone desperate enough to walk over a flaming cross to find
themselves \ I have become the sun-charted reminders of my ancestors;
no more dead than everyone else walking and breathing and talking

My bones more cathedral than capitalism could hope to give me in
exchanges for a *love* well lived / My life's work / are scrolls with secrets
ripped from harp strings & strum on / bolts shuttering into lightning
strike each time an owl blinks / but we know no magic here / in malls
unless it's a sale over 77%

Our forebears laugh into a sound that collapses the cosmos \ I laugh a
sound that breaks the fourth wall \ This epic of magic is sewn into the
fabric of time \ yet trapped by it \ *What a relief,* says some \ *What a
joke,* says others \ *What you say has power,* intones them who tap dance
on discordant strum

444

The planet does not need more
successful people. The planet
desperately needs more peace-
makers, healers, restorers, story-
tellers and lovers of all kinds.
—Dalai Lama

I am successful in learning that I'm not *conventionally* successful
I will not be the one who walks
into a business meeting
hair pressed to bone straightness

in a murdered suit, corpse stiff —
lips painted with the blood of my CFO
& drinking the tears of entry level employees
asked again how many millions I have made, all

while knowing I'm a cog in an oppressive system;
So, I will win less notoriety with capitalism
no medals or awards
but this golden heart

I set myself on fire to melt it down
& pour it out for strangers to smile
& feel less like the last sapling on barren land;
I am a cracked mirror

to reflect back some beauty
when you are a broken reflection
because healing is what we are all doing today
& you carry that torch inside you

to offer that shimmering essence in all that you do
& maybe you won't be successful
but you'll be the reason someone
learns to stay alive
& that is better than any high

than any award;
A gift worth fighting for –
Generously,
graciously alive.

neoteny

a consecrated maiden
frolics with eternal fountains of youth
in their fingertips;
whittling the birth of epochs
with over eager digits
& still never becoming jaded
to celestial marital procession—
but constantly showers petals
to pave primrose path;

Healing Humanity

i tried to practice my humanity
like dandelions trying to be sunflowers;
hoping i could package ether into the
incongruent mess of elements this body represents;

i've been too many deep emotions
when i should be shallow kiddie-pool conversation
i was a whale massive enough to swallow an ark;
Salvation tasted like soul food those time i became
distant when i should be close;
& i'm left wondering
if my humanity was never the issue

but all the ways my
captain save-a-hoe complex
has tricked me into death again

When she gave me a bottle of vitamin e for my self-inflicted scars
it was not to cover them & pretend they never existed;
it was to hasten the healing

i've found by separating the moon from her glow,
healing has always been an act of patience –

Knowing that
cadavers & cavalries
inhabited the same place while
learning to take space
in this rapidly expanding universe

exploding through time

creating yourself in that expansion
(once the scars heal)
& maybe that's humanity.

Plant Medicine

the Mugwort by the electric pole intones:
the secret to life
is learning to lose track of time
& love your growth.

the Roses down the lane answers:
it is okay if you did not love
your growth today,
you can try again
Tomorrow –

Envy, Thy Name Is Daffodil

Bright petal & petty;
blooming unexpectedly in groves
pollinated by popularity & gossip
but when plucked for bouquet,
it will choke the life out of its vase-mates

How did Envy get to be so severe;
that it does not wish to see others thrive?
aren't the violets and bluebells lovely too?
why when there's enough sunshine for all –

enough windowsill to invite more –

who said there was not enough room

for daffodils & roses too?

THE ILLUSION OF TIME

TICKING FORWARD;
BACKWARDS, ONLY IN MIND;
THIS, TO YOU GIVEN,
THE ILLUSION OF TIME.

PRESSED INTO PAGES,
HISTORIC PAGEANTRY SHOWN;
A PLAY ON CELESTIAL STAGE.
ATTENDANCE: OVERGROWN.

BEYOND THE EXPECTED.
THESE STORIES TAKE FLIGHT.
GIVEN BEYOND REASON,
TO THE THINGS OF THE NIGHT.

I DO NOT OBSERVE;
NOR DO I TAKE PART
OF RETELLING THESE TALES
FROM END, BACK TO START.

FOR ITS NOT TRUTH,
NOR LISTENS TO REASON.
TIME IS THIEF.
ITS MECHANISM'S TREASON.

I WILL NOT TELL YOU,
FOR THIS YOU WILL LEARN;
HOW TO ESCAPE THE VORTEX
WHEN IT IS YOUR TURN.

UNTIL NOW I MUST ASK YOU
TO GIVE AND TAKE HEART.
FOR YOUR JOURNEY IS LONG
AND YOU'RE STILL AT THE START.

DON'T BE QUICK TO GIVE UP.
DON'T TURN AWAY YOUR EAR.
FOR THIS PROPHECY IS NOT ONE
YOU'LL FINISH THIS YEAR.

IF YOU FIND YOURSELF RUSHING
OR FEELING MISLEAD.
TIME IS JUST AN ILLUSION.
IT'S ALL IN YOUR HEAD.

THERE IS NO COUNTDOWN.
NO UNEXPECTED FRIGHT.
JUST GO WHERE YOU ARE LEAD
AND WALK IN THE LIGHT.

4-D Dreamer

if a dreamer is dreaming a role within the dream;
is whatever that's happening the will of the dreamer
or the dream?
& why is no one waking up?

If Wishes Were Dollars, We'd All Be Rich

I wish, not for a fountain of youth nor for ruby slippers —
We've learned the grass is always greener on the
other side of the genie's lamp —
We do not wish for wishes but forge them like hot
pink daggers — ready to strong arm a new day out of
the gutters given to fig leaf hearts —

I wish the radical ideals of self-love & equality
turn antique rose pressed into the pages of history
because the revolution never stayed on the tip of the
tongue & it has already happened —

but if I were to wish anything let this ember gives
way to a blizzard across the equator because
everything has already shifted — that such wishes
become wholly unnecessary to you —

children of pomegranate & pines

who have spent so many nights wishing on stars to
just make it through the next morning & for the
nights you wished you didn't —

I wish you a world gentle enough that you spill the
excess out carelessly
for fountains of youth & greener grass.

The
Latter
Gospels

The Gospel of OSHUN

— as told by an uninitiated tongue

Oshun is offered only the best honey;
honey —
because it synthesizes growth
'cuz these roots have been
trapped far from homeland soil —

carted away to be planted
among thorn bushes but still blessed to thrive;
honey pot fastened to waist
because female pleasure
is portal to all creation;

She is The Great Mother
& lovers embodied —
all sticky sweet & feminine wiles
congruent with sweetening life
causing manifestations to flourish

Quietly mind your own manifestations,
child of the Great Mother —
sit in silence
& let her pour honey
out over you

If this is the end of your power,
let it be the beginning of Hers
ready to pour out those same offerings
over her children —
Is that not a Mother's love?

The Gospel of Medusa

There is no curse:
this transformation was always
a blessing begotten in love
giving venom & truth
loc'd up in serpent coil
what but truth
could harden heart & flesh
at first glance

what but the ability to see all
for as they are

One & all;
Kundalini swallowing itself —

for this,
there might be hissing yet,
this is the most peaceful
nest

a clutch of karma
sitting in the cosmic egg;
birthing multiplicity
for one who would learn all lessons
& clear out all debts

What wonderful venom
meant to protect
tied up in such normally useless follicles;
Fair sexed but battle-axed beauty
turned aegis of bronze

a signal of safety:
Justice's balanced sword
broad & bright
scales like snakes
through energetic light – ;;

Gospel of the Seen and not Heard

We are here; coughing up string;
wrenching & vomiting,
on all the things used to stitch
this voice box back together;
      Learning principles of vibration to form words

which shape worlds
break curses
& twist truthful tongues
back into themselves;
      Saliva swiped & salty
Ego-drenched
How could we not learn to taste
salvation from the swallowed tears
of torn homes?

      No longer showing up for riotous ruin or
fundamental clash;
the physics of when proton protagonists
No longer play part & collide with electrons
but break character & pull aside,
so imagination takes hold;
The scene comes out
all proud as prayer;
Look at you, finding your sunniest yourself —

If you can build & break
   children
      at the drop of a word,
         one truly prays you never
        tell them
          to be seen
            & ~~not~~ heard;

The Gospel of Maat is Renewed

Henceforth do we
members of the diaspora
whose people have been stolen & made orphaned
on the doors of colonizer cathedral
do recognize our right
as autonomous souls
– despite whatever chains this prison complex seeks to employ;

forewarn beneath sun and moon
cradled in the hips of Gaia
that we will make our hearts
light enough
to be buried in the field of reeds;

We accept our place as energetic sovereigns
sent to guard all portals of light on the planet
& in doing so
do recognize the light in all things
even in that of our opposition for it cannot be without light;

We, keepers of the night, do not allow light to
be extinguished called out to face atrocity & gave it a name

showed you the rituals done to keep you compliant
& watch the terror of it drive you mad
but, we do not accept madness or complacency
we demand dismantling of any thing sent
to hijack our consciousness

Shake fist to ruins of knowledge which has been stolen
& turn gaze inward to find it again

Facing an invincible a loaded deck
with cheerful determination
of lopsided dice
that know she will rebalance every scale

because we still carry our beloved dead in our ribs
they protect our heart & sing with each breath

So we observed the nine lords

but were not tempted by them

The Polarity of Victimhood

I had to stop thinking myself a
victim of sulking black cats leading my path
& rock away the bad luck blues; if
there is only one truth I know, it's
the universe is always conspiring in my favor

Whether with chisel or sledgehammer –
I have been, *am* being
carved – yet I too
have chisel fingers & a sledgehammer
mouth;

& the only one sabotaging me
is me; I am a victim
of nothing
but my own
mind;

Your Experience is Your Reward

In a place where you can grow exponentially; Be
a sunflower constantly craning upwards,
They always show up for themselves;
& follow the bliss towards brighter.
What a blessing –
to get to show up every day,
face the sun;
& bask in the experience of life.
How did we not know,
that we could live as simply as sunflowers?
Bright and vibrant,
surviving necessary gloom,
appreciating the gentle storm,
& waking again & again to glorious
sunshine –

FairyTale

If there was one thing I could gift to you
It's a fairy tale ending
Where your problems become as small as fairy fingernails
& disburse like dandelion seeds
What I mean is
I want you to be happy
Genuinely from your toes to your dandruff happy
Where it bubbles up like a rush
I want every day of your life to be a vacation
And you smile all the time to the point it's almost obnoxiously happy
But everyone around you is happy, too
So your smile never feels out of place or faked
I wish you
The best parking space every day happy
& really clear skin
Checked everything off on your to-do list but managed to nourish your
soul happy
I wish you always have the strength to brush your teeth
And days so bright you forget when depression makes the trek to the
bathroom an Everest climb
I would write you a fairy tale of never-ending happiness
I wish you such ridiculous
happiness
you never use another person as a marker
of your own worth but continue on your path keeping time with no one
but your own rhymes
I wish you and everyone pocks made of lucky ladybug print
I want everyone to be so stupidly happy

They don't think about hurting themselves
Not shooting down others in word and deed
Before turning that sword on themselves
Hot iron criticism
To the soft underbelly of dreams
But rather
They shine like smiling stars
Streaking bright across the firefly night sky
To guide the lost to better day
I want you to know what
Forgiveness smells like?
Is it like
Fresh grass after four nights of rain
Can you feel that calmness
That settles
The trembling of that fear to be seen
Know there's people turned wing chimes
Change resonates like beating drums
Shango calls us home
& it's always a joyful dance
How did we learn to move in time to life's dance,
If not practice
Learning to move through missteps

Every poem a heartbeat
Have you ever seen photographs pirouette
Fairy lights played on hair and heart
You are all fairy tale endings waiting for fresh starts
Life lives on in the poets
Children turned crone

Oral tradition of campfire wisdom
How you teach us life
How you teach us humanity
How you speak life into us

Why wouldn't you deserve a happy ending

How could you disbelieve your own magic, you beautiful fairytales
waiting to be told?

The

Vocations

Pilgrimage:

when daydreaming gratitude is a thought exercise outside of capitalism's grip

Daydreaming of days we don't trade for dollars

What's it like to live in a world
where free energy exists
but is an inaccessible bullseye safe,
guarded by corporations

I'm thankful to no longer consider myself
corporate property
but a saxophone solo that
no one asked for but
still feels right between ribs
when I say *I'd rather reclaim the rainforest,*
battle crocodiles and bull sharks than
let a CEO's snow day bankrupt
another summer squash farmer,

Each proletariat heart is a sunflower blooming at night –
I wish sometimes it didn't seem an unfair fight;

Somewhere between wildness & metropolis
a paradigm doesn't shift
but splits in two
I read tea leaves like a capitalism survival guide;

We rewrite its end & beginning daily
Capitalism's future has never been more unclear:
A cartouche carved in its memory
or puss-filled persists
festering ailment that we don't yet mass produce
overcharged medicines for?
Forgive me for saying: its future has always been in your hands.

Executioner's Plight

The gargoyle perched atop the church
has seen enough blood that it
could sour milk like lemonade that
lost its zest for everything
(most especially the sanctity of life).

It does not turn gaze to the heavenly
body of Neptune or
hope that sin will not be peacock proud;
Strutting as if it's right to bleach
burn orange boys into cotton & bones
was as god-given
as gems in quarry;

We do not meet stares long
enough to see that we cannot
be eye to eye on this.
His stony gaze ever forward,
stoic in the face at the atrocities
I want nothing more than to hide my face from.

I take aim:
archer & arrow ready to take eyes from
anything so stony that would watch the
children shuffled from homes to grave.

He stares:
sentient & unblinking;
I cannot blink enough tears to take aim,

I am not stone-hearted –
only I feel more gargoyle here;

Chiron in Cancer

When the healer needs healing,
they do not go
to those they have stitched
back together with tears & heart strings;
They do not go to the hands of humanity
which they adore and fear in equal measure;
They do not kiss the scabs
or wrap their arms around the scars of themselves;

They talk to the moon, the dead, and bits of rock;

When the healer needs healing,
they are too tired to explain
in all the ways they want
dawn to bloom into lilac bushes
and flags unfurling with potential;

They are too exhausted to wrap kindness
into a ribbon around a flower pot
& give it to you;

They have forgotten they are sanctuary & savior
because they did not save the world fast enough
and regenerate themselves
at the same time;

They are too busy fighting against themselves
to fight for you;

– and isn't that sad.

How they are tired of being a sad sentiment;
When they want to only give you hope
and vomit rainbows;

and tell you tomorrows are always beautiful
but will still sleep til noon;

Because when the healer need healing,
sometimes they don't talk to you.

When the healer needs healing,
they talk to the moon.

Shlimazel | Bad Luck

For those who find their snow day
met with upturned hot cocoa:
a spilled mess of smooth sailing
dripping off the laminate counter,
merging into a missed taxi
where you feel less than plum perfect
in your slow sunset day;

That is just fine.

Eclipse yourself not into despairing black hole,
sucking fun from the starry eyes like a ravenous vacuum;

There is no curse or cure:
blame no black cats
Your misfortune is also a slow sunset
that marks your spring mint morning that
is just around night's corner.

Sleep like luck has missed your address but
remembers the way back to you,
for surely it does;
Do not crack open your robin egg heart
over such a fleeting thing;
Dispel a 8ad 8reak in its own;

It will go
As it always does
sure as sunset
& sunrise again;

(What Will You Make Me continued)

Have you learned your limits
or are you still overextended limbs
seizing at things you cannot embrace you?
The gods are not dead
not sleeping
You, nocturnal dream-chaser.

are you tired of repeating someone else's story?
it's all about learning to ask the right questions:
what lays beyond the depths
beyond a ghost ship graveyard
of every hope lost at sea

There's no choice in being here just make the best of it, baby
there's no choice being here but make yourself better, baby
You will never be what we made: for that
Mercury story on your tongue is quick lighting,
lingering on the words you don't say:
This is what it means to be born into Spider's mouth
glowing radioactive, toxic shock & kryptonite

Recovery looks like:
not shying from your mirror at night;
Fearlessly refashioning yourself daily
from the pieces you found hiding in the
back of your closet,
worn & beloved–

finding what is
& has always been:

you

& this is what you have made yourself:
an idea in the physical —

A Panther Made of Pins & Needles

i have not learned to undo my mistakes
i have not learned to rewind the cracked record as it screeches & skips

my hands too concrete to keep sand dollar dreams
from crumbling in my grasp
i think about my twenties,
recount those lost years as one does a pitiful picnic basket
jettisoned into outer space —
too devoid of air for fire;
just frozen icy torrent where I wished baby's breath bloomed instead

i have not learned to undo my mistakes
but learned to face the prowling panther beneath my skin:

We cannot embrace each other, yet
We snarl less and less each passing day

We find peace in the inky morning –
looking forward to new days,
because today,
We do not think on our mistakes;

We think of ways to go
without baring fangs & fur;
on some days,
We even succeed;

We don't live in the skipped record's needled-grasp any longer –;

41°40'33" N 73°55'51" W

a south wind
moon
silver as scales
swims warm current towards autumn truths
It is single Damiana shoot dancing in the field
half-stoned
masonry arms
arched to meet a navy sky
A storm carried in Neptune's arms

what a way to break this stagnant humidity

what a way to breathe again

When I Am Older

I'll have learned to make a nest out of thorny brambles—that I will
no longer wear my heart on my sleeve in place of watches dripping
in panache

I don't think it matters that I have not figured out how yet.
Somehow, I'll have removed the iron gate around my home base heart;
so scared of someone who'll make a game of stealing it.

I think when I am older I'll stop looking for a dove to deliver letters
adorned with wax seal to decisions I haven't made yet;

I think when I am older I'll think of a halo less as a trophy earned but
rather a right of infancy and adjust others frequently to remind them it's
there, because when I am older,

I'll have realized there is an illusion of space & time and really there is
only ever here:

this margarita sunset
spiked with a love potion,
pressed to Life's lips;

To Conjure the Crone

If you find yourself looking to summon me,
come: in your best straw hat,
tribal head wrap or
bluebird silk bonnet

Offer plates of chicken & waffles
to my ancestral altar,
Do the cabbage patch in front of requests for council,
embellished with expensive wax seal

Burn it,
use sweet grass as kindling–
Pour two cups of coffee;
Yours, with half-and-half
Mine, out of a ginger-root mug

Dream in the wake of the monsoon
& decipher the meaning left behind cookie crumbs
like tossed bones or casting lots

If you need to summon me,
don't – but know,
I will meet you in whatever mountain town
pull you from whatever hollow cave
& set you on a new peak

If you do this:
set before me driftwood
from the Atlantic our ancestors traversed—
& carve it with your question;

leave me,
the inchworm from
the first spring day
the lilacs are in bloom;

& three Quartz
from the nearest quarry;
Sing my name – sweetly – like the sound
of the cello in June;

& beloved, I will come to you –

Luna Monet Sierra

Meet the Poet

Luna Monet Sierra is a rapidly decaying cluster of star matter trying their absolute best to be a functioning human on the third dimensional plane without losing themselves to it. They have a passion for self-expression.

While pretending to be a person, they have are a free-range transcendental poet with works published in *Silent Sparks Press*, *Free Verse Revolution*, and *Phantom Kangaroo*. Writing since they were in junior high, Luna has an extensive catalogue of poetry exploring everything from love to nature to dysphoria. Their unique voice brings a fresh perspective to the universe's whimsical nature.

While constantly seeking the wonder within the mundane, Luna studies the astrology and runs a discord server for Witches&Writers.

Colophon

Wider Perspectives Publishing regrets to have to announce that the ongoing Colophon page, used to tout artists published in books from WPP, has to be reworked. This is due to the growing library of fine writers coming out of, or even into, the Hampton Roads area of Virginia.

Daniel Garwood
Jada Hollingsworth
Tabetha Moon House
Travis Hailes- Virgo, thePoet
Nick Marickovich
Grey Hues
Rivers Raye
Madeline Garcia
Chichi Iwuorie
Symay Rhodes
Tanya Cunningham-Jones
    (Scientific Eve)
Terra Leigh
Raymond M. Simmons
Samantha Borders-Shoemaker
Taz Weysweete'
Jade Leonard
Darean Polk
Bobby K.
    (The Poor Man's Poet)
J. Scott Wilson (TEECH!)
Charles Wilson
Gloria Darlene Mann
Neil Spirtas
Jorge Mendez & JT Williams
Sarah Eileen Williams
Stephanie Diana (Noftz)
Shanya – Lady S.
Jason Brown (Drk Mtr)
Ken Sutton

Kailyn Rae Sasso
Crickyt J. Expression
Faith Griffin
Se'Mon-Michelle Rosser
Lisa M. Kendrick
Cassandra IsFree
Nich (Nicholis Williams)
Samantha Geovjian Clarke
Natalie Morison-Uzzle
Gus Woodward II
Patsy Bickerstaff
Edith Blake
Jack Cassada
Dezz

Catherine TL Hodges
Linda Spence-Howard
Maria April C.
Tony Broadway
Zach Crowe

Mark Willoughby
Martina Champion
... and others to come soon.

the Hampton Roads
  Perspectives) &
The Poet's Domain
are all WPP literary journals in cooperation with Scientific Eve or Live Wire Press

Check for those artists on FaceBook, Instagram, the Virginia Poetry Online channel on YouTube, and other social media.

www.ingramcontent.com/pod-product-compliance
Lightning Source LLC
Chambersburg PA
CBHW021223260626
47172CB00002B/568